VINEGAR TOM

by
CARYL CHURCHILL

SAMUEL FRENCH, INC.
45 WEST 25TH STREET   NEW YORK 10010
7623 SUNSET BOULEVARD HOLLYWOOD 90046
LONDON   TORONTO

IMPORTANT BILLING AND CREDIT REQUIREMENTS

All producers of VINEGAR TOM *must* give credit to the Author of the Play in all programs distributed in connection with performances of the Play and in all instances in which the title of the Play appears for purposes of advertising, publicizing or otherwise exploiting the Play and/or a production. The name of the Author *must* also appear on a separate line, in which no other name appears, immediately following the title, and *must* appear in size of type not less than fifty percent the size of the title type.

Vinegar Tom was written for Monstrous Regiment and was first presented at the Humberside Theatre, Hull, on 12 October 1976 with the following cast:

JOAN .... Mary McCusker
SUSAN............................... Sue Todd
ALICE............................ Gillian Hanna
GOODY .... Helen Glavin
BETTY .... Josefina Cupido
MARGERY...................... Linda Broughton
ELLEN............................ Chris Bowler
JACK................................ Ian Blower
MAN, DOCTOR, BELLRINGER,
PACKER............................ Roger Allam
KRAMER and
SPRENGER .... Chris Bowler and Mary McCusker

Directed by Pam Brighton
Designed by Andrea Montag
Music by Helen Glavin

VINEGAR TOM

SCENE ONE

MAN. Am I the devil?

ALICE. What, sweet?

MAN. I'm the devil. Man in black, they say, they always say, a man in black met me in the night, took me into the thicket and made me commit uncleaness unspeakable.

ALICE. I've seen men in black that's no devils unless clergy and gentlemen are devils.

MAN. Have I not got great burning eyes then?

ALICE. Bright enough eyes.

MAN. Is my body not rough and hairy?

ALICE. I don't like a man too smooth.

MAN. Am I not ice cold?

ALICE. In a ditch in November.

MAN. Didn't I lie on you so heavy I took your breath? Didn't the enormous size of me terrify you?

ALICE. It seemed a fair size like other men's.

MAN. Didn't it hurt you? Are you saying I didn't hurt you?

ALICE. You don't need be the devil, I been hurt by men. Let me go now, you're hurting my shoulder.

MAN. What it is, you didn't see my feet.

ALICE. You never took off your shoes. Take off your shoes if your feet's cloven.

5

MAN. If you come with me and give me body and soul, you'll never want in this world.

ALICE. Are you saying that as a man?

MAN. Am I saying it as the devil?

ALICE. If you're saying it as a man I'll go with you. There's no one round here knows me going to marry me. There's no way I'll get money. I've a child, mind, I'll not leave the child.

MAN. Has it a father?

ALICE. No, never had.

MAN. So you think that was no sin we did?

ALICE. If it was I don't care.

MAN. Don't say that.

ALICE. You'd say worse living here. Any time I'm happy someone says it's a sin.

MAN. There's some in London say there's no sin. Each man has his own religion nearly, or none at all, and there's women speak out too. They smoke and curse in the tavern and they say flesh is no sin for they are God themselves and can't sin. The men and women lie together and say that's bliss and that's heaven and that's no sin. I believe it for there's such changes.

ALICE. I'd like to go to London and hear them.

MAN. But then I believe with Calvin that few are saved and I am damned utterly. Then I think if I'm damned anyway I might as well sin to make it worthwhile. But I'm afraid to die. I'm afraid of the torture after. One of my family was burnt for a Catholic and they all changed to Protestant and one burnt for that too. I wish I was a Catholic and could confess my sins and burn them away in candles. I believe it all in turn and all at once.

ALICE. Would you take me to London? I've nothing to keep me here except my mother and I'd leave her.

MAN. You don't think I'm sent you by the devil? Sometimes I think the devil has me. And then I think there is no devil. And then I think the devil would make me think there was no devil.

ALICE. I'll never get away from here if you don't take me.

MAN. Will you do everything I say, like a witch with the devil her master?

ALICE. I'll do like a wife with a husband her master and that's enough for man or devil.

MAN. Will you kiss my arse like the devil makes his witches?

ALICE. I'll do what gives us pleasure. Was I good just now?

MAN. In Scotland I saw a witch burnt.

ALICE. Did you? A real witch? Was she a real one?

MAN. She was really burnt for one.

ALICE. Did the spirits fly out of her like black bats? Did the devil make the sky go dark? I've heard plenty tales of witches and I've heard some called witch, there's one in the next village some say and others say not, but she's nothing to see. Did she fly at night on a stick? Did you see her flying?

MAN. I saw her burnt.

ALICE. Tell then. What did she say?

MAN. She couldn't speak, I think. They'd been questioning her. There's wrenching the head with a cord. She came to the stake in a cart and men lifted her out, and the stake held her up when she was tied. She'd been in the boots you see that break the bones.

ALICE.   And wood was put round? And a fire lit just like lighting a fire? Oh, I'd have shrieked, I cry the least thing.

MAN.   She did shriek.

ALICE.   I long to see that. But I might hide my face. Did you hide your face?

MAN.   No, I saw it.

ALICE.   Did you like seeing it then?

MAN.   I may have done.

ALICE.   Will you take me with you, to London, to Scotland? Nothing happens here.

MAN.   Take you with me?

ALICE.   Please, I'd be no trouble.

MAN.   A whore? Take a whore with me?

ALICE.   I'm not that.

MAN.   What are you then? What name would you put to yourself? You're not a wife or a widow. You're not a virgin. Tell me a name for what you are.

ALICE.   You're not going? Stay a bit.

MAN.   I've stayed too long. I'm cold. The devil's cold. Back to my warm fire, eh?

ALICE.   Stay with me!

MAN.   Get away, will you.

ALICE.   Please.

MAN.   Get away. *(He pushes her and she falls.)*

ALICE.   Go to hell then, go to the devil, you devil.

MAN.   Cursing is it? I can outcurse you.

ALICE.   You foul devil, you fool, bastard, damn you, you devil!

MAN.   Devil take you, whore, whore, damned strumpet, succubus, witch!

ALICE. But come back. I'll not curse you. Don't you curse. We were friends just now.

MAN. You should have behaved better.

ALICE. Will I see you again?

MAN. Unless I see you first.

ALICE. But will I see you? How can I find you?

MAN. You can call on me.

ALICE. How? Where? How shall I call on you?

MAN. You know how to curse. Just call on the devil.

ALICE. Don't tease me, you're not the devil, what's your name?

MAN. Lucifer, isn't it, and Beelzebub.

ALICE. No, what's your name?

MAN. Darling was my name. and sweeting till you called me devil.

ALICE. I'll not call you devil, come back, what's your name?

MAN. You won't need to know it. You won't be seeing me.

SCENE TWO

JACK. The river meadow is the one to get.

MARGERY. I thought the long field up the hill.

JACK. No, the river meadow for the cattle.

MARGERY. But Jack, for corn. Think of the long field

full of wheat.

JACK. He's had a bad crop two years. That's why he can't pay the rent.

MARGERY. No, but he's got no cattle. We'd be all right.

JACK. If we took both fields.

MARGERY. Could we? Both?

JACK. The more we have the more we can afford.

MARGERY. And we'll pray God sends us sunshine.

JACK. Who's that down by the river?

MARGERY. That Alice, is it, wandering about?

JACK. I'm surprised Mother Noakes can pay her rent.

MARGERY. Just a cottage isn't much.

JACK. I've been wondering if we'll see them turned out.

MARGERY. I don't know why she's let stay. If we all lived like her it wouldn't be the fine estate it is. And Alice...

JACK. You can't blame Alice.

MARGERY. You can blame her. You can't be surprised. She's just what I'd expect of a girl brought up by Joan Noakes.

JACK. If we rent both fields, we'll have to hire a man to help with the harvest.

MARGERY. Hire a man?

JACK. That's not Alice.

MARGERY. It's not Miss Betty out by herself again?

JACK. I wouldn't be her father, not even to own the land.

MARGERY. That's a fine idea, hire a man.

JACK. She's coming here.

MARGERY. What we going to do?

JACK. Be respectful.

MARGERY. No, but shall we take her home? She's not meant to. She's still shut up in her room, everyone says.

JACK. I won't be sorry to see her.

MARGERY. I love to see her. She was always so soft on your lap, not like ours all hard edges. I could sit all afternoon just to smell her hair. But she's not a child, now, you can have run in and out and touch her. She's in trouble at home and we shouldn't help her do wrong.

JACK. We can't stop her, can we, if she walks in? *(They wait and in a moment BETTY does come in.)*

MARGERY. Miss Betty, how nice.

BETTY. I came to see you milking the cows.

JACK. We finished milking, miss. The cows are in.

BETTY. Is it that late?

MARGERY. You want to get home before dark.

BETTY. No, I don't. I want to be out in the dark. It's not late, it's dark in the day time. I could stay out for hours if it was summer.

JACK. If you want to come and see the farm, Miss Betty, you should ask your father to bring you one morning when he's inspecting the estate.

BETTY. I'm not let go where I like.

JACK. I've business with your father.

MARGERY. We're going to take on the river meadow for the cattle.

JACK. And the long field up the hill.

BETTY. I used to play here all day. Nothing's different. Have you still got Betty's mug?

MARGERY. That's right, she had her special mug.

BETTY. I milked the red cow right into it one day. I got milk in my eye.

JACK. She died, that red cow. But we've four new cows you've not seen.

MARGERY. Died last week. There's two or three cows died in the neighbourhood.

BETTY. I wish she hadn't.

JACK. That don't matter, losing one, we're doing well enough.

MARGERY. And you're doing well, I hear, miss.

BETTY. What?

MARGERY. I hear you're leaving us for better things.

BETTY. No.

MARGERY. I was only saying yesterday, our little Miss Betty that was and now to be a lady with her own house and—

BETTY. They lock me up. I said I won't marry him so they lock me up. Don't you know that?

MARGERY. I had heard something.

BETTY. I get out the window.

MARGERY. Hadn't you better have him, Betty, and be happy? Everyone hopes so. Everyone loves a wedding.

BETTY. Margery, can I stay here tonight?

MARGERY. They'd worry for you.

BETTY. Can I? Please?

JACK. There's no bed fit for you, miss.

BETTY. On my way here I climbed a tree. I could see the whole estate. I could see the other side of the river. I wanted to jump off. And fly.

MARGERY. Shall Jack walk home with you, miss, now it's getting dark?

SCENE THREE

JOAN. Alice?

ALICE. No need wake up, mum.

JOAN. You'll catch cold out all night in this weather.

ALICE. Don't wake up if it's only to moan at me.

JOAN. Who were you with?

ALICE. Did he wake up?

JOAN. No, not a sound.

ALICE. He's sleeping better. Not so much bad dreams.

JOAN. Come on, child, there's some broth left.

ALICE. I couldn't eat.

JOAN. You stay out half the night, you don't even enjoy it. You stay in with the boy. You sit by the fire with no one to talk to but old Vinegar Tomcat. I'll go out.

ALICE. You go out?

JOAN. Funny, isn't it? What would I do going out?

ALICE. I'll stay in if you like.

JOAN. Where would I go? Who wants an old woman?

ALICE. You want me to stay with you more?

JOAN. An old woman wandering about in the cold.

ALICE. Do you want some broth, mum?

JOAN. Who were you with this time? Any one I know?

ALICE. Oh mum, I'm sick of myself.

JOAN. If we'd each got a man we'd be better off.

13

ALICE. You weren't better off, mum. You've told me
often you're glad he's dead. Think how he used to
beat you.

JOAN. We'd have more to eat, that's one thing.

NOBODY SINGS

I met an old old woman
Who made my blood run cold
You don't stop wanting sex, she said,
Just because you're old.
  Oh nobody sings about it,
  but it happens all the time.

I could be glad of the change of life,
But it makes me feel so strange.
If your life is being wanted
Do you want your life to change?
  Oh nobody sings about it,
  but it happens all the time.

Do you want your skin to wrinkle
And your cunt get sore and dry?
And they say it's just your hormones
If you cry and cry and cry.
  Oh nobody sings about it,
  but it happens all the time.

Nobody ever saw me,
She whispered in a rage.
They were blinded by my beauty, now

They're blinded by my age.
　　　Oh nobody sings about it.
　　　but it happens all the time.

SCENE FOUR

MARGERY is churning.

JACK. Hurry up with that butter, woman.
MARGERY. Butter won't come.
JACK. There's other work to do.
MARGERY. Butter won't come.
JACK. You don't churn. You sit gossiping.
MARGERY. Who would I talk to?
JACK. I heard your voice now.
MARGERY. Mother Noakes.
JACK. Always hanging about.
MARGERY. Her girl's no better.
JACK. Was her girl here? No.
MARGERY. I told her be on her way. Mother Noakes.
JACK. You tell her.
MARGERY. I told her.
JACK. Get on now with the butter and don't be always gossiping. *(He goes.)*
MARGERY. *(Churns and sings very quietly.)*
Come butter come, come butter come. Johnny's standing at the gate waiting for a butter cake. Come butter come, come butter come. Johnny's standing at the gate waiting for a butter cake. Come butter come, come butter come.

Johnny's standing at the gate... *(She stops as she realizes JOAN NOAKES has come in and is standing behind her.)*

JOAN. Just passing by.

MARGERY. Again.

JOAN. I wonder could you lend me a little yeast? I've no yeast, see. I'm fresh out of yeast. I've no bread in the house and I thought, I thought ... I'll do a little baking now and brew a little beer maybe ... and I went to get some yeast and I've no yeast. Who'd have thought it? No yeast at all.

MARGERY. You'd be better without beer.

JOAN. I thought a little yeast as I was passing.

MARGERY. You get drunk. You should be ashamed.

JOAN. To bake a couple of little small loaves.

MARGERY. I've no yeast.

JOAN. A couple of little small loaves wouldn't take much yeast. A woman comfortable off with a fine man and a nice field and five cows and three pigs and plenty of apples that makes a good cider, bless you, Margery, many's the time ... you'd not grudge a neighbour a little loaf? Many's the good times, eh, Margery? I've my own flour, you know, I'm not asking for flour.

MARGERY. I gave you yeast last week.

JOAN. A little small crumb of yeast and God will bless you for kindness to your old neighbour.

MARGERY. You're not so badly off, Joan Noakes. You're not on the parish.

JOAN. If I was I'd be fed. I should be on relief, then I'd not trouble you. There's some on relief, better off than me. I get nothing.

MARGERY. What money you get you drink.

JOAN. If you'd my troubles, Margery, you'd be glad of a drink, but as you haven't, thank God, and lend me a little yeast like a good woman.

MARGERY. I've no yeast.

JOAN. I know you, Margery.

MARGERY. What do you know?

JOAN. I know you've got yeast. My eyes are old, but I see through you. You're a cold woman and getting worse and you'll die without a friend in this parish when if you gave yeast to your good neighbours everyone would bless you...

MARGERY. I've no yeast.

JOAN. But you don't give and they say what a mean bitter woman and curse you.

MARGERY. There's nobody curses me. Now get out of my dairy. Dirty old woman you are, smelling of drink, come in here day after day begging, and stealing, too, I shouldn't wonder...

JOAN. You shouldn't say that.

MARGERY. ....and your great ugly cat in here stealing the cream. Get out of my dairy.

JOAN. You'll be sorry you spoke to me like that. I've always been your friend, Margery, but now you'll find I'm not.

MARGERY. I've work to do. Now get out. I'm making my butter.

JOAN. Damn your butter to hell.

MARGERY. Will you get out?

JOAN. Devil take you and your man and your fields and your cows and your butter and your yeast and your beer and your bread and your cider and your cold face...

MARGERY. Will you go? *(JOAN goes. MARGERY churns.)*
Come butter come, come butter come. Johnny's stand-
ing at the gate waiting for a butter cake. Come butter...
It's not coming, this butter. I'm sick of it.

(JACK enters.)

JACK. What's all this? You're a lazy woman, you know
that? Times are bad enough. The little black calf don't
look well.

MARGERY. Butter won't come. Mother Noakes said
damn the butter to hell.

JACK. Lazy slut, get on with it.

MARGERY. Come butter come. Come butter come.
Come butter come. Come butter come. Come butter
come. Come butter... Mother Noakes come begging and
borrowing. She still got my big bowl I give her some eggs
in that time she was poorly. She makes out I've treated
her bad. I've been a good neighbour to that woman years
out of mind and no return. We'll get that bowl back off
her. Jack, do you hear me? Go over Mother Noakes and
get my bowl. And we'll heat a horseshoe red hot and put
it in the milk to make the butter come.

SCENE FIVE

SUSAN. Don't always talk of men.
ALICE. He knew what he was doing.

SUSAN. You'll know what he was doing in a few months.

ALICE. No, it never happens. The cunning woman put a charm inside me.

SUSAN. Take more than a charm to do me good.

ALICE. Not again? Does he know?

SUSAN. He wants it. I know the night it was. He said, 'Let's hope a fine child comes of it.'

ALICE. And what did you say?

SUSAN. Devil take it.

ALICE. What he say to that?

SUSAN. He don't like me swearing.

ALICE. But the baby's not a year.

SUSAN. Two weeks late, so.

ALICE. But the baby's not weaned.

SUSAN. The boy wasn't weaned when I fell for the baby.

ALICE. You could go see the cunning woman.

SUSAN. What for?

ALICE. She's a good midwife.

SUSAN. I don't want a midwife. I got my mother, anyway. I don't want to think about it. Nearly died last time. I was two days.

ALICE. Go and see the cunning woman. Just go see.

SUSAN. What for?

ALICE. She could say for certain.

SUSAN. I'm sure for certain.

ALICE. She could give you a charm.

SUSAN. They do say the pain is what's sent to a woman for her sins. I complained last time after churching, and he said I must think on Eve who brought the sin into the world that got me pregnant. I must think on how woman tempts man, and how she pays God with her pain having the baby. So if we try to get round the pain, we're going against God.

ALICE. I hate my body.

SUSAN. You mustn't say that. God sent his son—

ALICE. Blood every month, and no way out of that but to be sick and swell up, and no way out of that but pain. No way out of all that till we're old and that's worse. I can't bear to see my mother if she changes her clothes. If I was a man I'd go to London and Scotland and never come back and take a girl under a bush and on my way.

SUSAN. You could go to the cunning woman.

ALICE. What for?

SUSAN. Charm.

ALICE. What for?

SUSAN. Love charm bring him back.

ALICE. I don't want him back.

SUSAN. Did he look wonderful, more than anyone here, that he's got you so low?

ALICE. It was dark. I wouldn't know him again.

SUSAN. Not so much how he looked as how he felt.

ALICE. I could do with it now, I can tell you. I could do with walking across that field again and finding him there just the same. I want a man I can have when I want, not if I'm lucky to meet some villain one night.

SUSAN. You always say you don't want to be married.

ALICE. I don't want to be married. Look at you. Who'd want to be you?

SUSAN. He doesn't beat me.

ALICE. He doesn't beat you.

SUSAN. What's wrong with me? Better than you.

ALICE. Three babies and what, two, three times miscarried and wonderful he doesn't beat you.

SUSAN. No one's going to marry you because they know you here. That's why you say you don't want to be married — because no one's going to ask you round here, because they know you. *(They move apart.)*

JACK. *(He has been lingering in the background a while, and now comes up to ALICE.)* It's not you I've come to see.

ALICE. Never thought it was.

JACK. You should have done then.

ALICE. Why?

JACK. You know why.

ALICE. You've come to see my mum, have you?

JACK. I've business with her, yes. That's why I came.

ALICE. She's somewhere around. I'll get her.

JACK. No hurry. Wait a bit. Never seem to talk.

ALICE. Nothing to talk about.

JACK. I'm forgetting. I brought something. *(He gives her two apples.)*

ALICE. Thank you. What then?

JACK. Am I not handsome enough, is that it?

ALICE. I don't want trouble.

JACK. No one's to know.

ALICE. If I say you're not handsome enough, will you go away?

JACK. Alice, you must. I have dreams.

ALICE. You've a wife.

JACK. I'm no good to my wife. I can't do it. Not these three months. It's only when I dream of you or like now talking to you—

ALICE. Mum. There's someone to see you.

JACK. Alice, have some pity—

ALICE. Do you hear me? Mum? She'll be out to see you. *(She moves away.)*

(JOAN enters.)

JOAN. What's the matter?

JACK. I've come for the bowl.

JOAN. Bowl? Bowl?

JACK. Bowl my wife gave you some eggs in, you ungrateful old hag.

JOAN. You're asking for the bowl? You think I wouldn't give you back your bowl? You think I'm stealing your bowl? When have I ever kept anything? Have your bowl. I'll get your bowl and much good may it do you.

JACK. Then get it, damn you, and quick or you'll feel my hand. *(JOAN goes.)*

ALICE. Why treat her like that?

JACK. Don't speak to me. Let me get the bowl and go.

ALICE. And don't come back.

JACK. Alice, I'd be good to you. I'm not a poor man. I could give you things for your boy...

ALICE. Go away to hell.

(JOAN enters.)

JOAN. Here's your bowl, Jack, and the devil go with it. Get away home and I hope you've more trouble there than I have here.

JACK. I'll break your neck if you speak to me.

JOAN. You lift your hand to me, may it drop off.

ALICE. Go home away to hell, man. *(JACK goes.)*

JOAN. Away to hell with him. Never liked the man. Never liked the wife.

ALICE. Don't think on them, mum. They're not worth your time. Go in by the fire, go on, go in and be warm. *(JOAN goes. SUSAN approaches.)* Nobody likes my mother. That's what it is why nobody wants me.

SUSAN. I'm sorry for what I said, Alice.

ALICE. Going to see the cunning woman then?

SUSAN. Are you going for a love charm?

ALICE. It's something to do, isn't it? Better than waiting and waiting for something to happen. If I had a charm I could make him just appear in front of me now, I'd do anything. Will you come? *(ALICE gives SUSAN an apple.)*

SUSAN. I'll keep you company then. Just tell her my trouble. There's no harm.

OH DOCTOR

Oh, doctor, tell
me, make me well.
What's wrong with me
The way I am?
I know I'm sad
I may be sick.

I may be bad.
Please cure me quick,
oh doctor.

SCENE SIX

BETTY tied to a chair. The DOCTOR is about to bleed her arm.

BETTY. Why am I tied? Tied to be bled. Why am I bled? Because I was screaming. Why was I screaming? Because I'm bad. Why was I bad? Because I was happy. Why was I happy? Because I ran out by myself and got away from them and— Why was I screaming? Because I'm bad. Why am I bad? Because I'm tied. Why am I tied? Because I was happy. Why was I happy? Because I was screaming.

DOCTOR. Hysteria is a woman's weakness. Hysteron, Greek, the womb. Excessive blood causes an imbalance in the humours. The noxious gasses that form inwardly every month rise to the brain and cause behaviour quite contrary to the patient's real feelings. After bleeding you must be purged. Tonight you shall be blistered. You will soon be well enough to be married.

OH DOCTOR

Where are you taking my skin?

Where are you putting my bones?
I shut my eyes and I opened wide,
But why is my heart on the other side?
Why are you putting my brain in my cunt?
You're putting me back all back to front.

Stop looking up me with your metal eye.
Stop cutting me apart before I die.
Stop. put me back.
Stop, put me back.
Put back my body.

Who are you giving my womb?
Who are you showing my breath?
Tell me what you whisper to nurse.
Whatever I've got, you're making it worse.
I'm wide awake, but I still can't shout.
Why can't I see what you're taking out?

Stop looking up me with your metal eye.
Stop cutting me apart before I die.
Stop, put me back.
Stop, put me back.
Put back my body.

Oh, doctor, tell
me, make me well.
What's wrong with me
the way I am?
I know I'm sad
I may be sick.

I may be bad.
Please cure me quick,
oh doctor,
What's wrong with me the way I am?
What's wrong with me?

I want to see myself.
I want to see inside myself.
Give me back my head.
I'll put my heart in straight.
Let me out of bed now.
I can't wait
To see myself.
Give me back my body.
I can see myself.

SCENE SEVEN

MARGERY. Jack, Jack, come quick — Jack.
JACK. What's the matter now?
MARGERY. The calves. Have you seen the calves?
JACK. What's the woman on about?
MARGERY. The calves are shaking and they've a terrible stench, so you can't go near them and their bellies are swollen up. *(JACK goes off.)* There's no good running. There's nothing you can do for them. They'll die like the red cow. You don't love me. Damn this stinking life to hell. Calves stinking and shaking there. No good you

going to see, Jack. Better stand and curse. Everything dying on us. Aah. What's that? Who's there? Get out, you beast, get out. *(She throws her shoe.)* Jack, Jack.

JACK. *(Comes back.)* Hold your noise.

MARGERY. That nasty old cat of Mother Noakes. I'll kill that cat if I get it, stinking up my clean dairy, stealing my cream. Where's it gone?

JACK. Let it go.

MARGERY. What you think of those calves then? Nothing to be done is there? What can we do? Nothing. Nothing to be done. Can't do nothing. Oh. Oh.

JACK. Now what is it?

MARGERY. Jack!

JACK. What is it? Don't frighten me, woman.

MARGERY. My head, oh, my stomach. Oh, Jack, I feel ill. *(She sits on the ground.)*

JACK. Get up, woman. It's no time. There's things to do.

MARGERY. Nothing.

JACK. Lie there a bit then. You'll maybe feel better. I can hardly stir myself. What have I done to deserve it? Why me? Why my calves shaking? Why my wife falling down?

MARGERY. It's passing now.

JACK. Why me?

MARGERY. That was a terrible pain. I still feel it. I'm shaking, look.

JACK. Other people sin and aren't punished so much as we are.

MARGERY. We must pray to God.

JACK. We do pray to God, and he sends afflictions.

MARGERY. It must be we deserve it somehow, but I don't know how. I do my best. I do my best, Jack, God knows, don't I, Jack? God knows I do my best.

JACK. Don't other people sin? Is it just me?

MARGERY. You're not a bad man, Jack.

JACK. I must be the worst man.

MARGERY. No, dear.

JACK. Would God send all this to a good man? Would he? It's my sins those calves shaking and stinking and swelling up their bellies in there.

MARGERY. Don't talk so.

JACK. My sins stinking and swelling up.

MARGERY. Unless it's not God.

JACK. How can I bear it?

MARGERY. If it's not God.

JACK. What?

MARGERY. If it's not God sends the trouble.

JACK. The devil?

MARGERY. One of his servants. If we're bewitched, Jack, that explains all.

JACK. If we're bewitched...

MARGERY. Butter not coming. Calves swelling. Me struck in the head.

JACK. Then it's not my sins. Good folk get bewitched.

MARGERY. Good folk like us.

JACK. It can happen to anyone.

MARGERY. Rich folk can have spells against them.

JACK. It's good people the witches want to hurt.

MARGERY. The devil can't bear to see us so good.

JACK. You know who it is?

MARGERY. Who?

JACK. The witch. Who it is.

MARGERY. Who?

JACK. You know who.

MARGERY. She cursed the butter to hell.

JACK. She cursed me when I got the bowl.

MARGERY. She said I'd be sorry I'd spoken to her.

JACK. She wished me trouble at home.

MARGERY. Devil take your man and your cows, she said that, and your butter. She cursed the calves see and she's made them shake. She struck me on the head and in the stomach.

JACK. I'll break her neck.

MARGERY. Be careful now, what she might do.

JACK. I'm not afraid of an old witch.

MARGERY. You should be. She could kill you.

JACK. I'll kill her first.

MARGERY. Wait, Jack. Let's meet cunning with cunning. What we must do is get the spell off.

JACK. She's not going to take it off for asking. She might for a few hard knocks.

MARGERY. No, wait, Jack. We can take the spell off and never go near her. Serve her right.

JACK. What we do then? Burn something?

MARGERY. Burn an animal alive, don't we? Or bury it alive. That takes witchcraft off the rest.

JACK. Burn the black calf then shall we? We'll get some straw and wood and put it in the yard and the calf on top and set it on fire.

MARGERY. Will it walk?

JACK. Or I'll carry it.

MARGERY. It stinks terrible.

JACK. Stink of witchcraft it is. Burn it up.

MARGERY. We must pray to God to keep us safe from the devil. Praying's strong against witches.

JACK. We'll pray God help us and help ourselves too.

MARGERY. She'll see the fire and smell it and she'll know we're fighting her back, stinking old witch, can't hurt us.

SOMETHING TO BURN

What can we do, there's nothing to do,
about sickness and hunger and dying.
What can we do, there's nothing to do,
nothing but cursing and crying.
> Find something to burn.
> Let it go up in smoke.
> Burn your troubles away.

Sometimes it's witches, or what will you choose?
Sometimes it's lunatics, shut them away.
It's blacks and it's women and often it's jews.
We'd all be quite happy if they'd go away.
> Find something to burn.
> Let it go up in smoke.
> Burn your troubles away.

SCENE EIGHT

ELLEN. Take it or leave it, my dear, it's one to me. If you want to be rid of your trouble, you'll take it. But only you know what you want.

SUSAN. It's not what I came for.

ALICE. Of course it is.

SUSAN. I wanted to know for certain.

ALICE. You know for certain.

SUSAN. I want a charm against pain.

ELLEN. I'll come as your midwife if you send for me near the time and do what I can, if that's all you want.

ALICE. She wants to be rid of it. Well, do you want it?

SUSAN. I don't want it but I don't want to be rid of it. I want to be rid of it, but not do anything to be rid of it.

ELLEN. If you won't do anything to help yourself you must stay as you are.

SUSAN. I shall pray to God.

ALICE. It's no sin. You just give yourself the drink.

SUSAN. Oh, I don't know.

ELLEN. Let her go home. She can come back. You have your charm safe, Alice? I could do more if you could come at the young man and give him a potion I'd let you have.

ALICE. If I could come at him he wouldn't need potion.

ELLEN. And you're sure you've nothing of his?

ALICE. He gave me nothing.

ELLEN. A few hairs or a drop of blood makes all the difference. It's part of him and the powers can work on it to call him.

ALICE. I'll pull a few hairs out next time I've a lover. Come on, Susan.

ELLEN. For your heartache I'll give you these herbs to boil up in water and drink at night. Give you a sound sleep and think less of him.

ALICE. Don't want to think less of him.

ELLEN. You have your sleep. There'll be other men along if not that one. Clever girl like you could think of other things.

ALICE. Like what?

ELLEN. Learn a trade.

ALICE. Nothing dangerous.

ELLEN. Where's the danger in herbs?

ALICE. Not just herbs.

ELLEN. Where's the danger in healing?

ALICE. Not just healing, is it?

ELLEN. There's powers, and you use them for healing or hurt. You use them how you like. There's no hurt if you're healing so where's the danger? You could use them. Not everyone can.

ALICE. Learn the herbs?

ELLEN. There's all kinds of wisdom. Bit by bit I'd teach you.

ALICE. I'd never thought.

ELLEN. There's no hurry. I don't want you unless it's what you want. You'll be coming by to leave a little something for me in a few days, since I have to live and wouldn't charge you. You can tell me how you've got on with your young man and what you're thinking.

ALICE. Yes, I'll be coming by. Goodnight then. What are you standing there for, Susan?

SUSAN. Maybe I'll take some potion with me. And see when I get home whether I take it.

ELLEN. Don't be afraid if it makes you very sick. It's to do you good.

SCENE NINE

BETTY. I don't know what I'm here for. I've had so much treatment already. The doctor comes every day.

ELLEN. You know what you're here for.

BETTY. The doctor says people like you don't know anything. He thinks he's cured me because I said I would get married to stop them locking me up. But I'll never do it.

ELLEN. Do you want a potion to make you love the man?

BETTY. I'd rather have one to make him hate me so he'd leave me alone. Or make him die.

ELLEN. The best I can do for you is help you sleep. I won't harm him for you, so don't ask. Get some sleep and think out what you want.

BETTY. Can I come again sometimes just to be here? I like it here.

ELLEN. Come when you like. I don't charge but you'll bring a little present.

BETTY. I'll give you anything if you can help me.

ELLEN. Come when you like.

SCENE TEN

ELLEN. I'm not saying I can't do anything. But if I can't, it's because you've left it too late.

JACK. Lift your hand to me, she said, may it drop off. Then next day it went stiff.

MARGERY. We want to be certain. I've talked to others and they've things against her too.. She's cursed and scolded two or three, and one's lame and the other lost her hen. And while we were talking we thought of her great cat that's always in my dairy, stinking it up and stealing the cream. Ah what's that, I said crying out, didn't I, and that was the cat, and I was struck down with a blow inside my head. That's her familiar sent her by Satan.

JACK. I've seen a rat run out of her yard into ours and I went for it with a pitchfork and the spikes were turned aside and nearly went in my own foot by her foul magic. And that rat's another of her imps.

MARGERY. But you don't like to think it of your neighbour. Time was she was neighbourly enough. If you could tell us it was true, we could act against her more certain in our minds.

JACK. I shouted at her over the fence, I said I'll have you hanged you old strumpet, burnt and hanged, and she cursed me again.

MARGERY. We burnt a calf alive to save our calves but it was too late. If I knew for certain it was her I'd be easier.

ELLEN. I've a glass here, a cloudy glass. Look in the glass, so, and see if any face comes into it. *(She gives them a mirror.)*

MARGERY. Come on, Jack, don't be afraid.

JACK. I don't like it.

MARGERY. Come on, it's good magic to find a witch.

ELLEN. Look in the glass and think on all the misfortunes you've had and see what comes.

MARGERY. Nothing yet. Do you see anything?

JACK. No.

MARGERY. Nothing still.

JACK. Don't keep talking.

MARGERY. Look.

JACK. What?

MARGERY. Did something move in the glass? My heart's beating so.

JACK. It's too dark.

MARGERY. No. Look.

JACK. I did see something.

MARGERY. It's the witch.

JACK. It's her sure enough.

MARGERY. It is, isn't it, Jack? Mother Noakes, isn't it?

JACK. It was Mother Noakes in that glass.

ELLEN. There then. You have what you came for.

MARGERY. Proves she's a witch then?

ELLEN. Not for me to say one's a witch or not a witch. I give you the glass and you see in it what you see in it.

JACK. Saw Mother Noakes.

MARGERY. Proves she's a witch.

ELLEN. Saw what you come to see. Is your mind easy?

SCENE ELEVEN

JACK. Want to ask you something private. It's about my... *(He gestures, embarrassed.)* It's gone. I can't do anything with it, haven't for some time. I accepted that. But now it's not even there, it's completely gone. There's a girl bewitched me. She's the daughter of that witch. And I've heard how witches sometimes get a whole boxful and they move and stir by themselves like living creatures and the witch feeds them oats and hay. There was one witch told a man in my condition to climb a tree and he'd find a nest with several in it and take which he liked, and when he took the big one she said no, not that one, because that one belongs to the parish priest. I don't want a big one, I want my own back, and this witch has it.

ELLEN. You'd better go and ask her nicely for it.

JACK. Is that all you can say? Can't you force her to give it me?

ELLEN. It's sure to come back. You ask the girl nicely,

she'll give it you back. I'll give you a little potion to take.

JACK. Kill her else.

SCENE TWELVE

JOAN. That's a foul stink. I don't know how you can stay there. Whatever is it?

MARGERY. Do you know why you've come?

JOAN. I was passing.

MARGERY. Why were you passing?

JOAN. Can't I pass by your door now? Time was it was always open for me.

MARGERY. And what's that?

JOAN. A foul stink. Whatever are you making? I thought I'd come and see you as I was passing. I don't want any trouble between us. I thought, come and see her, make it all right.

MARGERY. You come to see me because of that. That's my piss boiling. And two feathers of your chicken burning. It's a foul stink brings a witch. If you come when I do that, proves you've a spell on me. And now I'll get it off. You know how?

JOAN. Come and see you. Make it all right.

MARGERY. Blood you, that's how. *(MARGERY scratches JOAN'S head.)*

JOAN. Damn you, get away.

MARGERY. Can't hurt me now. And if that doesn't

bring the spell off I'll burn your thatch.

IF EVERYBODY WORKED AS HARD AS ME

If everybody worked as hard as me,
if our children's shirts are white,
if their language is polite,
if nobody stays out late at night,
Oh, happy family.
Oh, the country's what it is because
the family's what it is because
the wife is what she is
to her man.
Oh I do all I can.
Yes, I do all I can.
I try to do what's right,
so I'll never be alone and afraid in the night
And nobody comes knocking at my door in the night.
The horrors that are done will not be done to me.

Nobody loves a scold,
nobody loves a slut,
nobody loves you when you're old,
unless you're someone's gran.
Nobody loves you
unless you keep your mouth shut.
Nobody loves you
if you don't support your man.
Oh you can,
oh you can
have a happy family.

If everybody worked as hard as me,
sometimes you'll be bored,
you'll often be ignored,
but in your heart you'll know you are adored.

Oh, happy family.
Your dreams will all come true.
You'll make your country strong.
Oh the country's what it is because
the family's what it is because
the wife is what she is
to her man.
Oh please do all you can.
Yes, please do all you can,
Oh, please don't do what's wrong,
so you'll never be alone and afraid in the night.
So nobody comes knocking at your door in the night.
So the horrors that are done will not be done to you.

Yes you can.
Yes you can.
Oh the country's what it is because
the family's what it is because
the wife is what she is
to her man.

SCENE THIRTEEN

SUSAN. You're sure it was him? You said you wouldn't know him.

ALICE. I did when I saw him.

SUSAN. Riding? Couldn't see him close.

ALICE. Close enough to be spattered with his mud. He saw me.

SUSAN. But he didn't show he knew you.

ALICE. Pretended not to.

SUSAN. It wasn't him.

ALICE. It was him.

SUSAN. And you don't know the beautiful lady?

ALICE. I'll know her again. Scratch her eyes if I come at her.

SUSAN. What was she wearing?

ALICE. What was she wearing? How should I know? A fine rich dress made her beautiful, I suppose. Are you trying to plague me?

SUSAN. Was he in black still?

ALICE. Blue velvet jacket.

SUSAN. Blue velvet.

ALICE. Yes, damn you, I said that before. Are you stupid? *(silence)* For God's sake, now what is it? Are you crying? Shouldn't I be crying?

SUSAN. It's not your fault, Ally. I cry all the time.

ALICE. You're still weak, that's what it is. It's the blood you lost. You should rest more.

SUSAN. I don't want him to know.

ALICE. Doesn't he know?

SUSAN. He may guess but I don't dare ask. He was out all day that day and I said I'd been ill, but not why.

ALICE. It's done anyway.

SUSAN. Can't be undone.

ALICE. You're not sorry now?

SUSAN. I don't know.

ALICE. You'd be a fool to be sorry.

SUSAN. I am sorry. I'm wicked. You're wicked. *(She cries.)*

ALICE. Oh, Susan, you're tired out, that's all. You're not wicked. You'd have cried more to have it. All the extra work, another baby.

SUSAN. I like babies.

ALICE. You'll have plenty more, God you'll have plenty. What's the use of crying?

SUSAN. You were crying for that lover.

ALICE. I'm not now. I'd sooner kill him. If I could get at him. If thoughts could get at him he'd feel it.

SUSAN. I'm so tired, Ally.

ALICE. Do you think it's true thoughts can reach someone?

SUSAN. What are you thinking of?

ALICE. Like if I had something of his, I could bring him. Or harm him.

SUSAN. Don't try that.

ALICE. But I've nothing of his. I'd have to make a puppet.

SUSAN. Don't talk so. Oh, don't, Alice, when I'm so tired.

ALICE. Does it have to be like? Is it like just if you say it's like?

SUSAN. Alice!

ALICE. If I get this wet mud, it's like clay. There should be at least a spider or some ashes of bones, but mud will do. Here's a man's shape, see, that's his head and that's arms and legs.

SUSAN. I'm going home. I'm too tired to move.

ALICE. You stay here and watch. This is the man. We know who though we don't know his name. Now here's a pin, let's prick him. Where shall I prick him? Between the legs first so he can't get on with his lady.

SUSAN. Alice, stop.

ALICE. Once in the head to drive him mad. Shall I give him one in the heart? Do I want him to die yet? Or just waste till I please.

SUSAN. Alice... *(SUSAN tries to get the mud man, it falls on the ground and breaks.)*

ALICE. Now look. You've broken him up. You've killed him.

SUSAN. I haven't.

ALICE. All in pieces. Think of the poor man. Come apart.

SUSAN. I didn't. Alice, I didn't. It was you.

ALICE. If it was me, I don't care.

SUSAN. Alice, what have you done? Oh Alice, Alice.

ALICE. It's not true, stupid. It's not him.

SUSAN. How do you know?

ALICE. It's a bit of mud.

SUSAN. But you said.

ALICE. That's just words.

SUSAN. But—

ALICE. No. I did nothing. I never do anything. Might be better if I did. *(They sit in silence.)* You're crying again. Here, don't cry. *(ALICE holds SUSAN while she cries.)*

SUSAN. Little clay puppet like a tiny baby not big enough to live and we crumble it away.

(JACK enters.)

JACK. Witch.

ALICE. Are you drunk?

JACK. Give it back.

ALICE. What?

JACK. Give it back.

ALICE. What now, Jack?

JACK. Give it me back. You know. You took it from me these three months. I've not been a man since. You bewitched me. You took it off me.

ALICE. Is he mad?

SUSAN. What is it?

ALICE. Susan's ill, will you leave us alone?

JACK. Everyone comes near you is ill. Give it back, come on, give it back.

ALICE. How can I?

JACK. She said speak nicely to you. I would, Alice, if you were good to me. I never wanted this. Please, sweet good Alice, give it back.

ALICE. What? How can I?

JACK. Give it me. *(He grabs her round the neck. SUSAN screams.)*

ALICE. Damn you!

SUSAN. You'll kill her—

JACK. Give it me—

SUSAN. Let her go, she'll give it you whatever it is, you'll kill her, Jack.

JACK. *(He lets go.)* Give it me then. Come on.

SUSAN. Wait, she can't move, leave her alone.

JACK. Give it me.

ALICE. *(Puts her hand between his thighs.)* There. It's back.

JACK. It is. It is back. Thank you, Alice. I wasn't sure you were a witch till then. *(He goes.)*

SUSAN. What you doing, Alice? Alice?

ALICE. *(Turns to her.)* It's nothing. He's mad. Oh my neck, Susan. Oh, I'd laugh if it didn't hurt.

SUSAN. Don't touch me. I'll not be touched by a witch.

SCENE FOURTEEN

BELLRINGER. Whereas if anyone has any complaint against any woman for a witch, let them go to the townhall and lay their complaint. For a man is in town that is a famous finder of witches and has had above thirty hanged in the country round and he will discover if they are or no. Whereas if anyone has any complaint against any woman for a witch, let them go...

MARGERY. Stopped the butter.

JACK. Killed the calves.

MARGERY. Struck me in the head.

JACK. Lamed my hand.

MARGERY. Struck me in the stomach.

JACK. Bewitched my organ.

MARGERY. When I boiled my urine she came.

JACK. Blooded her and made my hand well.

MARGERY. Burnt her thatch.

JACK. And Susan, her friend, is like possessed screaming and crying and lay two days without speaking.

MARGERY. Susan's baby turned blue and its limbs twisted and it died.

JACK. Boy threw stones and called them witch, and after he vomited pins and straw.

MARGERY. Big nasty cat she has in her bed and sends it to people's dairies.

JACK. A rat's her imp.

MARGERY. And the great storm last night brought a tree down in the lane, who made that out of a clear sky?

PACKER. I thank God that he has brought me again where I am needed. Don't be afraid any more. You have been in great danger but the devil can never overcome the faithful. For God in his mercy has called me and shown me a wonderful way of finding out witches, which is finding the place on the body of the witch made insensitive to pain by the devil. So that if you prick that place with a pin no blood comes out and the witch feels nothing at all.

(PACKER and GOODY take JOAN, and GOODY holds her, while PACKER pulls up her skirts and pricks her legs.

JOAN curses and screams throughout. PACKER and GOODY abuse her: a short sharp moment of great noise and confusion.)

GOODY. Hold still you old witch. Devil not help you now, no good calling him. Strong for your age, that's the devil's strength in her, see. Hold still, you stinking old strumpet...

PACKER. Hold your noise, witch, how can we tell what we're doing? Ah, ah, there's for you devil, there's blood, and there's blood, where's your spot, we'll find you out Satan...

JOAN. Damn you to hell, oh Christ help me! Ah, ah, you're hurting, let go, damn you, oh sweet God, oh you devils, oh devil take you...

PACKER. There, there, no blood here, Goody Haskins. Here's her spot. Hardly a speck here.

GOODY. How she cries the old liar, pretending it hurts her.

PACKER. There's one for hanging, stand aside there. We've others to attend to. Next please, Goody.

(GOODY takes ALICE. PACKER helps, and her skirts are thrown over her head while he pricks her. She tries not to cry out.)

GOODY. Why so much blood?

PACKER. The devil's cunning here.

GOODY. She's not crying much, she can't feel it.

PACKER. Have I the spot though? Which is the spot? There. There. There. No, I haven't the spot. Oh, it's tiring work. Set this one aside. Maybe there's others will speak against her and let us know more clearly what she is. *(ALICE is stood aside.)* If anyone here knows anything more of this woman why she might be a witch, I charge them in God's name to speak out, or the guilt of filthy witchcraft will be on you for concealing it.

SUSAN. I know something of her.

PACKER. Don't be shy then girl, speak out.

ALICE. Susan, what you doing? Don't speak against me.

SUSAN. Don't let her at me.

ALICE. You'll have me hanged. *(SUSAN starts to shriek hysterically.)*

GOODY. Look, she's bewitched.

MARGERY. It's Alice did it to her.

ALICE. Susan, stop.

SUSAN. Alice. Alice. Alice.

PACKER. Take the witch out and the girl may be quiet. *(GOODY takes ALICE off. SUSAN stops.)*

MARGERY. See that.

JACK. Praise God I escaped such danger.

SUSAN. She met with the devil, she told me, like a man in black, she met him in the night and did uncleaness with him, and ever after she was not herself but wanted to be with the devil again. She took me to a cunning woman and they made me take a foul potion to destroy the baby in my womb and it was destroyed. And the cunning woman said she would teach Alice her wicked magic, and she'd have powers and not everyone could learn that, but Alice could because she's a witch, and the cunning woman gave her something to call the devil, and she tried to call him, and she made a puppet, and stuck pins in, and tried to make me believe that was the devil, but that was my baby girl, and next day she was sick and her face blue and limbs all twisted up and she died. And I don't want to see her.

PACKER. These cunning women are worst of all. Everyone hates witches who do harm but good witches they go to for help and come into the devil's power without knowing it. The infection will spread through the whole country if we don't stop it. Yes, all witches deserve death, and the good witch even more than the bad one. Oh God, do not let your kingdom be overrun by the devil. And you, girl, you went to this good witch, and you destroyed the child in your womb by witchcraft, which is a grievous offence. And you were there when this puppet was stuck with pins, and consented to the death of your own baby daughter?

SUSAN. No, I didn't. I didn't consent. I never wished her harm. Oh if I was angry sometimes or cursed her for crying, I never meant it. I'd take it back if I could have her back. I never meant to harm her.

PACKER. You can't take your curses back, you cursed her to death. That's two of your children you killed. And what other harm have you done? Don't look amazed, you'll speak soon enough. We'll prick you as you pricked your babies.

SCENE FIFTEEN

GOODY. There's no man finds more witches than Henry Packer. He can tell by their look, he says, but of course he has more ways than that. He's read all the books and he's travelled. He says the reason there's so much witchcraft in England is England is too soft with its witches, for in Europe and Scotland they are hanged and burned and if they are not penitent they are burnt alive, but in England they are only hanged. And the ways of discovering witches are not so good here, for in other countries they have thumbscrews and racks and the bootikens which is said to be the worst pain in the world, for it fits tight over the legs from ankle to knee and is driven tighter and tighter till the legs are crushed as small as might be and the blood and marrow spout out and the bones are crushed and the legs made unserviceable forever. And very few continue their lies and denials then. In England we haven't got such thorough ways, our ways are slower but they get the truth in the end when a fine skilful man like Henry Packer is onto them. He's well worth the twenty shillings a time, and I get the same, which is very good of him to insist on and well worth it though some folk complain and say, 'what, the price of a cow, just to have a witch hanged?' But I say to them think of the expense a witch is to you in the damage she does to pro-

49

perty, such as a cow killed one or two pounds, a horse maybe four pounds, besides all the pigs and sheep at a few shillings a time, and chickens at sixpence all adds up. For two pounds and our expenses at the inn, you have all that saving, besides knowing you're free of the threat of sudden illness and death. Yes, it's interesting work being a searcher and nice to do good at the same time as earning a living. Better than staying home a widow. I'd end up like the old women you see, soft in the head and full of spite with their muttering and spells. I keep healthy keeping the country healthy. It's an honour to work with a great professional.

SCENE SIXTEEN

BETTY. I'm frightened to come any more. They'll say I'm a witch.

ELLEN. Are they saying I'm a witch?

BETTY. They say because I screamed that was the devil in me. And when I ran out of the house they say where was I going if not to meet other witches. And some know I come to see you.

ELLEN. Nobody's said it yet to my face.

BETTY. But the doctor says he'll save me. He says I'm not a witch, he says I'm ill. He says I'm his patient so I can't be a witch. He says he's making me better. I hope I can be better.

ELLEN. You get married, Betty, that's safest.

BETTY. But I want to be left alone. You know I do.

ELLEN. Left alone for what? To be like me? There's no doctor going to save me from being called a witch. Your best chance of being left alone is marry a rich man, because it's part of his honour to have a wife who does nothing. He has his big house and rose garden and trout stream, he just needs a fine lady to make it complete and you can be that. You can sing and sit on the lawn and change your dresses and order the dinner. That's the best you can do. What would you rather? Marry a poor man and work all day? Or go on as you're going, go on strange? That's not safe. Plenty of girls feel like you've been feeling, just for a bit. But you're not one to go on with it.

BETTY. If it's true there's witches, maybe I've been bewitched. If the witches are stopped, maybe I'll get well.

ELLEN. You'll get well, my dear, and you'll get married, and you'll tell your children about the witches.

BETTY. What's going to happen? Will you be all right?

ELLEN. You go home now. You don't want them finding you here. *(BETTY goes.)* I could ask to be swum. They think the water won't keep a witch in, for Christ's baptism sake, so if a woman floats she's a witch. And if she sinks they have to let her go. I could sink. Any fool can sink. It's how to sink without drowning. It's whether they get you out. No, why should I ask to be half drowned? I've done nothing. I'll explain to them what I do. It's healing, not harm. There's no devil in it. If I keep calm and explain it, they can't hurt me.

IF YOU FLOAT

If you float you're a witch
If you scream you're a witch
If you sink, then you're dead anyway.
If you cure you're a witch
Or impure you're a witch
Whatever you do, you must pay.
Fingers are pointed, a knock at the door,
You may be a mother, a child or a whore.
If you complain you're a witch
Or you're lame you're a witch
Any marks or deviations count for more.
Got big tits you're a witch
Fall to bits you're a witch
He likes them young, concupiscent and poor.
Fingers are pointed, a knock at the door,
They're coming to get you, do you know what for?

So don't drop a stitch
My poor little bitch
If you're making a spell
Do it well.
Deny it you're bad
Admit it you're mad
Say nothing at all
They'll damn you to hell.

SCENE SEVENTEEN

*ALICE is tied up, sitting on the floor. GOODY is eating and
yawning.*

GOODY. You'd better confess, my dear, for he'll have
you watched night and day and there's nothing makes a
body so wretched as not sleeping. I'm tired myself. It's
for your own good, you know, to save you from the devil.
If we let you stay as you are, you'd be damned eternally
and better a little pain now than eternal... *(She realizes
ALICE is nodding to sleep and picks up a drum and bangs it loud-
ly. She gives it several bangs to keep ALICE awake.)*

(PACKER comes in.)

GOODY. She's an obstinate young witch, this one, on
her second night. She tires a body out.
PACKER. Go and sleep, Goody. I'll watch her a
while.
GOODY. You're a considerate man, Mr. Packer. We
earn our money. *(She goes.)*
PACKER. I'm not a hard man. I like to have my confes-
sion so I'm easy in my mind I've done right.
ALICE. Where's my boy?
PACKER. Safe with good people.
ALICE. He wants me.
PACKER. He's safe from the devil, where you'll never
come.

ALICE. I want him.

PACKER. Why won't you confess and make this shorter?

ALICE. It isn't true.

PACKER. Tell me your familiars. Tell me your imps' names. I won't let them plague you for telling. God will protect you if you repent.

ALICE. I haven't any. *(PACKER drums.)* I want my boy.

PACKER. Then you should have stayed home at night with him and not gone out after the devil.

ALICE. I want him.

PACKER. How could a mother be a filthy witch and put her child in danger?

ALICE. I didn't.

PACKER. Night after night, it's well known.

ALICE. But what's going to happen to him? He's only got me.

PACKER. He should have a father. Who's his father? Speak up, who's his father?

ALICE. I don't know.

PACKER. You must speak.

ALICE. I don't know.

PACKER. You must confess. *(He drums.)*

ALICE. Oh my head. Please don't. Everything's drumming.

PACKER. I'll watch. Your imps will come to see you.

ALICE. Drumming.

PACKER. *(Suddenly stops.)* Ah. Ah. What's this? A spider. A huge black one. And it ran off when it saw a godly man. Deny if you can that spider's one of your imps.

ALICE. No.

PACKER. Then why should it come? Tell me that.

ALICE. I want my boy.

PACKER. Why? Why do you keep on about the boy?
Who's the father? Is the devil his father?

ALICE. No, no, no.

PACKER. I'll have the boy to see me in the morning. If
he's not the devil's child he'll speak against you. *(ALICE
cries.)* I'll watch you. I've watched plenty of witches and
hanged them all. I'll get that spider too if it comes
back.

SCENE EIGHTEEN

GOODY is shaving SUSAN under the arm.

GOODY. There, that's the second arm done, and no
mark yet. Devil hides his marks all kinds of places. The
more secret the better he likes it. Though I knew one
witch had a great pink mark on her shoulder and neck so
everyone could see. And a woman last week with a big
lump in her breast like another whole teat where she
sucked her imps, a little black one she had and a little
white one and kept them in wool in a bottle. And when I
squeezed it first white stuff came out like milk and then
blood, for she fed those horrid creatures on milk and
blood and they sucked her secret parts in the night too.
Now let's see your secret parts and see what the devil does

there. *(She makes SUSAN lie down, and pulls up her skirt to shave her.)*

(PACKER comes in.)

PACKER. What devil's marks?

GOODY. No need to shave the other for she has three bigs in her privates almost an inch long like great teats where the devil sucks her and a bloody place on her side where she can't deny she cut a lump off herself so I wouldn't find it.

PACKER. Such a stinking old witch I won't look myself. Is there nothing here?

GOODY. She's clean yet but we'll shave her and see what shameful thing's hidden.

PACKER. Though a mark is a sure sign of a witch's guilt having no mark is no sign of innocence for the devil can take marks off.

JOAN. And the devil take you.

PACKER. You'll be with the devil soon enough.

JOAN. And I'll be glad to see him. I been a witch these ten years. Boys was always calling after me and one day I said to a boy, 'Boy, boy you call me witch but when did I make your arse to itch.' And he ran off and I met a little grey kitling and the kitling said, 'You must go with me' and I said, 'Avoid, Satan.' And he said, 'You must give me your body and soul and you'll have all happiness.' And I did. And I gave him my blood every day, and that's my old cat Vinegar Tom. And he lamed John Peter's son that's a cripple this day, that was ten years ago. And I had two more imps sent me crept in my bed in the night sucked my privy parts so sore they hurt me and wouldn't leave me. And I asked them to kill Mary Johnson who crossed me and she wasted after. And everyone knows Annie that had fits and would gnash her teeth and took six strong men to hold her. That was me sent those fits to her. My little imps are like moles with four feet but no tails and a black colour. And I'd send them off and they'd come back in the night and say they did what I said. Jack is lucky I didn't bewitch him to death and Margery, but she was kind to me long ago. But I killed their cows like I killed ten cows last year. And the great storm and tempest comes when I call it and strikes down trees. But now I'm in prison my power's all gone or I'd call down thunder and twist your guts.

PACKER. Is there any reason you shouldn't be hanged?

JOAN. I'm with child.

GOODY. Who'd believe that?

SCENE NINETEEN

JOAN and ELLEN are hanged while MARGERY prays.

MARGERY. Dear God, thank you for saving us. Let us live safe now. I have scrubbed the dairy out. You have shown your power in destroying the wicked, and you show it in blessing the good. You have helped me in my struggle against the witches, help me in my daily struggle.

Help me work harder and our good harvests will be to your glory. Bless Miss Betty's marriage and let her live happy. Bless Jack and keep him safe from evil and let him love me and give us the land, amen.

SCENE TWENTY

JOAN and ELLEN hanging.

SUSAN. Alice, how can you look? Your poor mother. You're not even crying.

ALICE. She wasn't a witch. She wouldn't know how.

SUSAN. Alice, she was.

ALICE. The cunning woman was, I think. That's why I was frightened of her.

SUSAN. I was a witch and never knew it. I killed my babies. I never meant it. I didn't know I was so wicked. I didn't know I had that mark on me. I'm so wicked. Alice, let's pray to God we won't be damned. If we're hanged, we're saved, Alice, so we mustn't be frightened. It's done to help us. Oh God, I know now I'm loathsome and a sinner and Mr. Packer has shown me how bad I am and I repent. I never knew that but now I know and please forgive me and don't make me go to hell and be burnt forever—

ALICE. I'm not a witch.

SUSAN. Alice, you know you are. God, don't hear her say that.

ALICE. I'm not a witch. But I wish I was. If I could live
I'd be a witch now after what they've done. I'd make wax
men and melt them on a slow fire. I'd kill their animals
and blast their crops and make such storms, I'd wreck
their ships all over the world. I shouldn't have been
fightened of Ellen, I should have learnt. Oh if I could
meet with the devil now I'd give him anything if he'd give
me the power. There's no way for us except by the devil.
If I only did have magic, I'd make them feel it.

LAMENT FOR THE WITCHES

Where have the witches gone?
Who are the witches now?
Here we are.

All the gentle witches' spells
blast the doctors' sleeping pills.
The witches hanging in the sky
haunt the courts where lawyers lie.
Here we are.

They were gentle witches
with healing spells.
They were desperate witches
with no way out but the other side of hell.

A witch's crying in the night
switches out your children's light.
All your houses safe and warm
are struck at by the witches' storm.
Here we are.

Where have all the witches gone?
Who are the witches now?
Here we are.

They were gentle witches
with healing spells
They were desperate witches
with no way out but the other side of hell.
Here we are.

Look in the mirror tonight.
Would they have hanged you then?
Ask how they're stopping you now.
Where have the witches gone?
Who are the witches now?
Ask how they're stopping you now.
Here we are.

SCENE TWENTY-ONE

SPRENGER. He's Kramer.

KRAMER. He's Sprenger.

KRAMER and SPRENGER. *(together)* Professors of Theology.

KRAMER. delegated by letters apostolic

SPRENGER. (here's a toast, non-alcoholic).

KRAMER. Inquisitors of heretical pravities

SPRENGER. we must fill those moral cavities

KRAMER. so we've written a book

SPRENGER. *Malleus Maleficarum*

KRAMER. *The Hammer of Witches.*

SPRENGER. It works like a charm

KRAMER. to discover witches

SPRENGER. and torture with no hitches.

KRAMER. Why is a greater number of witches found in the fragile feminine sex than in men?

SPRENGER. Why is a greater number of witches found in the fragile feminine sex than in men?

KRAMER. 'All wickedness is but little to the wickedness of a woman.' Ecclesiastes.

SPRENGER. Here are three reasons, first because

KRAMER. woman is more credulous and since the aim of the devil is to corrupt faith he attacks them. Second because

SPRENGER. women are more impressionable. Third because

KRAMER. women have slippery tongues and cannot conceal from other women what by their evil art they know.

SPRENGER. Women are feebler in both body and mind so it's not surprising.

KRAMER. In intellect they seem to be of a different nature from men—

SPRENGER. like children.

KRAMER. Yes.

SPRENGER. But the main reason is

KRAMER and SPRENGER. *(together)* she is more carnal than a man

KRAMER. as may be seen from her many carnal

abominations.

SPRENGER. She was formed from a bent rib.

KRAMER. and so is an imperfect animal.

SPRENGER. Fe mina, female, that is fe faith minus without

KRAMER. so cannot keep faith.

SPRENGER. A defect of intelligence.

KRAMER. A defect of inordinate passions.

SPRENGER. They brood on vengeance.

KRAMER and SPRENGER. *(together)* Wherefore it is no wonder they are witches.

KRAMER. Women have weak memories.

SPRENGER. Follow their own impulses.

KRAMER. Nearly all the kingdoms of the world have been overthrown by women

SPRENGER. as Troy, etc.

KRAMER. She's a liar by nature

SPRENGER. vain

KRAMER. more bitter than death

SPRENGER. contaminating to touch

KRAMER. their carnal desires

SPRENGER. their insatiable malice

KRAMER. their hands are as bands for binding when they place their hands on a creature to bewitch it with the help of the devil.

SPRENGER. To conclude.

KRAMER. All witchcraft

SPRENGER. comes from carnal lust

KRAMER. which is in woman

KRAMER and SPRENGER. *(together)* insatiable.

KRAMER. It is no wonder there are more women than

men found infected with the heresy of witchcraft.

SPRENGER. And blessed be the Most High, which has so far preserved the male sex from so great a crime.

EVIL WOMEN

Evil women
Is that what you want?
Is that what you want to see?
On the movie screen
Of your own wet dream
Evil women.

If you like sex sinful, what you want is us.
You can be sucked off by a succubus.
We had this man, and afterwards he died.

Does she do what she's told or does she nag?
Are you cornered in the kitchen by a bitching hag?

Satan's lady, Satan's pride.
Satan's baby, Satan's bride,
A devil woman's not easily satisfied.

Do you ever get afraid
You don't do it right?
Does your lady demand it
Three times a night?
If we don't say you're big
Do you start to shrink?
We earn our own money
And buy our own drink.

Did you learn you were dirty boys, did you learn
Women were wicked to make you burn?
Satan's lady, Satan's pride,
Satan's baby, Satan's bride,
Witches were wicked and had to burn.

Evil women
Is that what you want?
Is that what you want to see?
In your movie dream
Do they scream and scream?
Evil women
Evil women
Women.

AUTHOR'S NOTES

I first met Monstrous Regiment on a march, abortion I think, early in 1976. I ran into Chris Bowler and she introduced me to some of the others. Chris said the company were thinking they would like to do a play about witches; so was I, though it's hard now to remember what ideas I was starting from. I think I had already read *Witches, Midwives and Nurses* by Barbara Ehrenreich and Deirdre English. Certainly it had a strong influence on the play I finally wrote.

Soon I met the whole company to talk about working with them. They gave me a list of books they had read and invited me to a rehearsal of *Scum*. I left the meeting exhilarated. I'd been writing plays for eighteen years, half my life: for the stage as a student, then a lot of radio, then in 1972 *Owners* followed by *Moving Clocks Go Slow, Objections to Sex and Violence,* all done at the Royal Court; a few weeks earlier I had finished *Traps*. All this work had been completely solitary — I never discussed my ideas while I was writing or showed anyone anything earlier than a final polished draft. So this was a new way of working, which was one of its attractions. Also a touring company, with a wider audience; also a feminist company — I felt briefly shy and daunted, wondering if I would be acceptable, then immensely happy and stimulated by the discovery of shared ideas and the enormous energy and feeling of possibilities in the still new company.

I was about to do a play for Joint Stock, who excited me for some of the same reasons, some different. There

65

wasn't a lot of time, and the two plays, *Vinegar Tom* and *Light Shining in Buckinghamshire,* overlapped both in time and ideas. All I knew at this point about the Joint Stock project was that it was going to be about the English Revolution in the 1640s, what people had wanted from it, and particularly the millenial expectations of the Ranters. A lot of what I was learning about the period, religion, class, the position of women, was relevant to both plays.

Over Easter on Dartmoor I read books, Monstrous Regiment's suggestions and others I had found; rapidly left aside the interesting theory that witchcraft had existed as a survival of suppressed pre-Christian religions and went instead for the theory that witchcraft existed in the minds of its persecutors, that 'witches' were a scapegoat in times of stress like jews and blacks. I discovered for the first time the extent of Christian teaching against women and saw the connections between medieval attitudes to witches and continuing attitudes to women in general. The women accused of witchcraft were often those on the edges of society, old, poor, single, sexually unconventional; the old herbal medical tradition of the cunning woman was suppressed by the rising professionalism of the male doctor. I didn't base the play on any precise historical events, but set it rather loosely in the mid-seventeenth century, partly because it was the time of the last major English witchhunts, and partly because the social upheavals, class changes, rising professionalism and great hardship among the poor were the context of the kind of witchhunt I wanted to write about; partly of course because it was the period I was already reading for Joint Stock. One of the things that struck me reading the detailed accounts of witch trials in Essex *(Witchcraft in Tudor and Stuart England*, Macfarlane) was how petty and everyday the witches' offences were, and how different the atmosphere of actual English witchhunts seemed to be from my received idea, based on slight knowledge of the European witchhunts and films and fiction, of burnings, hysteria and sexual orgies. I wanted to write a play about witches with no witches in it; a play not about evil, hysteria and possession by the devil but about poverty, humiliation and prejudice, and how the women accused of witchcraft saw themselves.

I met Monstrous Regiment again, talked over the ideas I had so far, and found the same aspects of witchcraft appealed to them too. Then I went off and wrote a first draft of the play, very quickly, in about three days. I may have written one or two songs at this stage but not all of them. The company were happy to accept this first draft and leave rewriting till after my work with Joint Stock, which was lucky as in May I started the Joint Stock workshop. June-July I wrote *Light Shining,* rehearsed through August, and it opened at the Edinburgh festival. Then I met Monstrous Regiment again. Helen Glavin had been working on the music for the songs during the summer. I worked on the text again, expanding it slightly. It was only at this stage that Josefina Cupido joined the company and I wrote in the character of Betty, who didn't exist before and who filled a need that had come up in discussion for a character under pressure to make a conventional marriage. 'Why am I tied' was originally from a scene that never fitted in *Light Shining,* part of

Hoskins' early life! During rehearsals I remember Gillian Hanna who played Alice, pointing out that Alice's child was mentioned early in the play but not after she was in prison, and I sat at a table in the corner of the rehearsal room and wrote the scene where Packer asks if it is the devil's child. It was a very easy and enjoyable co-operation with the company. My habit of solitary working and shyness at showing what I wrote at an early stage had been wiped out by the even greater self-exposure in Joint Stock's method of work. And our shared view of what the play was about and our commitment to it made rewriting precise and easy. I particularly enjoyed working on the songs with Helen Glavin, and again this was something I hadn't done before — but did again the next year, working on Monstrous Regiment's cabaret *Floorshow* with Michelene Wandor and Bryony Lavery. By the time *Traps* was done at the Theatre Upstairs in January 1977 it seemed more than a year since I had written it. Though I still wanted to write alone sometimes, my attitude to myself, my work and others had been basically and permanently changed by the two shows I had written since, for Joint Stock and Monstrous Regiment.

PRODUCTION NOTE

When *Vinegar Tom* was originally published by Theatre Quarterly I included almost no stage directions. I always prefer to keep them to a minimum and as I was with the company throughout rehearsal there was no need to write anything down. A couple of productions since then, in San Francisco and at Smith College, Mass., made me realise that I should have pointed out that the songs, which are contemporary, should if possible be sung by actors in modern dress. They are not part of the action and not sung by the characters in the scenes before them. In the original company all the actors could sing so it was no problem for some members of the company to be out of costume at any time to be in the band. Obviously this may not always be possible. But it is essential that the actors are not in character when they sing the songs.

Another point is that the pricking scene is one of humiliation rather than torture and that Packer is an efficient professional, not a sadistic maniac.

It's important that Kramer and Sprenger are played by women. Originally they were played by Chris Bowler and Mary McCusker, who as Ellen and Joan had just been hanged, which seems to be an ideal doubling. They played them as Edwardian music hall gents in top hats and tails, and some of the opening rhymes and jokes are theirs. The rest of the scene is genuine Kramer and Sprenger, from their handbook on witches and women, *Malleus Maleficarum, the Hammmer of Witches*.

Caryl Churchill

MONSTROUS REGIMENT NOTES

Vinegar Tom was Monstrous Regiment's second production. The idea for a play about witchcraft came out of the initial meetings we'd had the previous year. The list of subjects for shows was enormous, but witchcraft was always high on it. At first our knowledge of the subject was very patchy, some people had done a fair amount of reading, for others it was restricted to Hammer Horrors. But all agreed in dismissing the traditional image of the evil old crone/buxom young temptress with the pointed hat and deadly potions — we smelled a rat. We were just about to go into rehearsal with our first play, *Scum*, when we met up with Caryl Churchill and discovered — wonderful coincidence — that we all wanted to do the same play. We wasted no time in commissioning her.

We were delighted with the first draft. It said so much in so few words. We found it full of humour, passion, and above all good parts for women! There were no rewrites in the normal sense, no cuts, but we decided to introduce another character. We wanted to show the pressures and constraints of that very narrow seventeenth century society on a young noblewoman, Betty, materially better off, but with little more choice or power over her life than Alice or Susan.

Working with Caryl on the script, and later during rehearsals, was the company's first real experience of working closely with a woman writer. It hadn't been possible in the same way with Claire Luckham on *Scum* — she lives in Liverpool and had family commitments which restricted the amount of time she could spend with us. It was a very exciting and creative period for us. The need for all of us to speak the truth about these persecuted women, fired and united us, and there was a great feeling of joy in the shared enterprise. In putting the character of Betty into the play, for instance, the progress from ideas and feelings to sections of dialogue seemed amazingly quick and painless. First we discussed what we wanted to say with the character, and what scenes were needed for it. Then, whilst we rehearsed something else in one part of the rehearsal room, Caryl sat in a corner and wrote the extra scenes. At the end of the day, bingo, two new scenes. We thought to ourselves 'Ah, so *this* is what it's like working with a woman writer,' and fondly imagined all our productions rolling out with equal ease and enjoyment.

Looking back, it's difficult to remember at what point the songs appeared. There may have been one or two lyrics in the first draft — it was certainly always our intention to include as much music as possible in the play. Since the beginning there had been a composer/singer/pianist in the company, Helen Glavin, and Josefina Cupido was just about to join us — having been lurking about on the edges of the company for some time. We all felt a frustration with the way we had seen music used so often in the theatre. We were determined that ours should be original in style, and should have an intellectual and creative life of its own — pushing the action along almost as much as the dialogue, not simply existing as a decoration or breathing space in the plot. Accordingly during rehearsals we decided with Caryl, that the music should be performed in modern dress and pro-

vide a contemporary commentary on the action. The
instruments (piano, congas and guitar) and the voices
were all acoustic, so Helen was able to compose music
that was in keeping with the period yet could strongly
embrace twentieth century idioms.

The writer/group collaboration was so close, with
Caryl attending all rehearsals, it isn't easy to pinpoint
where specific ideas came from. One production ele-
ment that certainly came from the company was the deci-
sion to cast the women's parts against what would
normally be regarded as 'type'. We wanted to challenge
those stereotypes, and in addition give ourselves the
opportunity as actors to expand into parts normally for-
bidden to us because we were too young/old/thin/fat.

The play received a very interesting reaction. It
gathered a different, perhaps more feminist/women's
audience than *Scum.* Some men in particular were upset
by it. With *Scum* (about the Paris commune of 1870-71)
they felt included in the struggle of the women laundry
workers, with this they were definitely placed outside the
experience of the female characters. Some people felt
accused by the songs, which in their manner of presenta-
tion — as well as in the lyrics and music — were direct
and uncompromising. It wasn't our intention to make
people feel accused or blamed in a simplistic way, but
neither did we want to let them off the hook, or allow
them to distance themselves emotionally from the events
of the play because they were distant historically. At the
other end of the spectrum we were accused of being too
heterosexual, some women found the male/female love-
making of the first scene offensive. This was the com-

pany's first taste of critical reaction to our politics from other women, and it was very chastening. The climate of the media, and to some extent public reaction, towards feminism has changed so much during the life-time of Monstrous Regiment. It has gone from unpopular to trendy to passé, and reaction to our work has zig-zagged with it. At first (when there were very few feminist/women's groups) it often felt as though we were urgently required to embody every shade of feminist belief, and whenever we represented one person we negated another.

The reaction from reviewers on the whole was very favourable, even if they weren't keen on the politics of the play, they couldn't deny the strength of the writing. When Ned Chaillet of *The Times* described it as 'a picture slightly different from the one handed down through legend and historical records', we knew we'd succeeded.

Two last notes. The Pricking: We used stage blood only in the pricking scene with Packer and Alice, and here it was very effective — causing several people to faint or be helped retching from the theatre. The Hanging: We decided to make this as realistic as possible, using a wooden frame and climbing harnesses under Mary and Chris' nightdresses — which were hooked on to trick nooses. Nevertheless it was widely believed that they were dummies, more attention being paid to the Alice/Susan scene going on in front, and Mary and Chris are still complaining about damage to their spines.

Monstrous Regiment

② Doctors Song

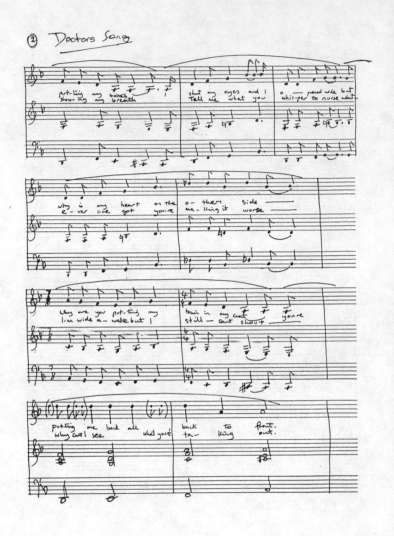

③ Doctors Song

Voices ② & ②

Voices (?)(?) stop look-ing up me with your me-tal eye, stop cut-ting me a—

put be-fore I die   stop—put me back,   stop—put me back —.

put—back my bo— dy   voice ①
1st time D.S.
O—doc-tor   voices ① ① & ①
2nd time
a tempo   want to

see — my-self   I   want to   see in-side my-self.

④ Doctors Song

(5) Doctors Song

Fine

① <u>Something to Burn</u>

no-thing but curs-ing and cry ing Find
hap-py if they'd go a-way

Chorus

f Some-thing to burn let it go up in smoke Burn your

troubles a-way Find

Some-thing to burn let it go up in smoke Burn your

③ Something to Burn

Dal Segno.

troubles a- way

loss you keep your mouth shut. No-bo-dy loves you if you don't support your man-Oh you

can-Oh you can — have a hap-py fa — mi — ly 2) If

cresc

to 2nd time at coda. D.S. 🔁

Coda

cresc —

can — . The cow-boys that it is be-cause the wife is that she is to her man

f

Fine

② Witches Lament

cresc. witches hanging in the sky,
houses safe and warm are
haunt the courts where law-yers
struck at by the witches

f lie
storm

Humming
(1)
(2) Here we

are

(1)
(2) They were gen- tle witch- es with

③ Witches Lament

heal _____ -ing spells,

mf They were desperate witch- es with
cresc

no way out but the o-ther side — of
cresc   *cresc*

Da Capo

f hell _____

(5) Witches Lament

rit

p are . . . . p Here we are . . . . Fire

③ Evil Women

③ Evil Women

died

3X

do   what she's told or   does she   nag?   are   you

cor—nered in the kit·chen by a bitching   hag?

Harmony

Sa—tans la—dy,   Sa— tans pride,   Sa—tans ba—by

(4) Evil Women

2nd time — al ⊕

Sa- tans bride ! De- vil wo- mans not eas- il- y sat- is —

fied

1) Do you ever get afraid
2) That you don't do it right
3) Does your lady demand it
4) Three times a night?
   if we don't say you're big
5) Do you start to shrink
6) We earn our own money
   and buy our own drink.

One line
a bar—
spoken over
congas +
piano.

8

Did you learn you were dirty boys did you

learn. Wo- man, were wicked to, make you burn.

D.S.

(5) Evil Women